JAN 1 7

THE BOAT RACE

BY RACHEL BACH

amicus readers

Say Hello to Amicus Readers.

You'll find our helpful dog, Amicus, chasing a ball—to let you know the reading level of a book.

1

Learn to Read
High frequency words and close photo-text matches introduce familiar topics and provide ample support for brand new readers.

2

Read Independently
Some repetition is mixed with varied sentence structures and a select amount of new vocabulary words are introduced with text and photo support.

3

Read to Know More
Interesting facts and engaging art and photos give fluent readers fun books both for reading practice and to learn about new topics.

Amicus Readers and Amicus Ink are imprints of Amicus
P.O. Box 1329, Mankato, MN 56002
www.amicuspublishing.us

Library of Congress Cataloging-in-Publication Data
Names: Bach, Rachel, author.
Title: The boat race / by Rachel Bach.
Description: Mankato, Minnesota : Amicus, [2017] | Series: Let's Race.
Identifiers: LCCN 2015041490 (print) | LCCN 2015047707 (ebook) | ISBN 9781607539117 (library binding) | ISBN 9781681510354 (eBook) | ISBN 9781681521305 (paperback)
Subjects: LCSH: Motorboat racing--Juvenile literature.
Classification: LCC GV835.9 .B33 2017 (print) | LCC GV835.9 (ebook) | DDC 797.1/4--dc23
LC record available at http://lccn.loc.gov/2015041490

Editor: Wendy Dieker
Designer: Tracy Myers
Photo Researcher: Rebecca Bernin

Photo Credits: Chatchai Somwat/Alamy cover; Imaginechina/Corbis 3; homydesign/Shutterstock 4-5; Henrique NDR Martins/iStock 7; Getty 8-9; Martin P Wilson/Demotix/Corbis 11; Owe Andersson/Alamy 12-13; Andrew Shlykoff/Alamy 15; Jason Kirk/Alamy 16

Printed in the United States of America.

HC 10 9 8 7 6 5 4 3 2 1
PB 10 9 8 7 6 5 4 3 2 1

The green flag goes up.
The power boat race is on!

Sam drives
the white boat.
Zoom!

Fans watch
on the beach.
Who will win?

The boats go for 15 laps. Val is in the lead.

Oh no! A big wave!
The red boat flips over.

The driver is okay.

Dan is the fastest!
He wins!

PARTS OF A POWER BOAT

engine

cockpit

hull